3

JAMES
5

PERCY
6

MEET ALL THESE FRIENDS IN BUZZ BOOKS:

Thomas the Tank Engine
The Animals of Farthing Wood
Biker Mice From Mars
James Bond Junior
Fireman Sam
Joshua Jones
Rupert
Babar

First published 1992 by Buzz Books
an imprint of Reed Children's Books
Michelin House, 81 Fulham Road, London SW3 6RB
and Auckland, Melbourne, Singapore and Toronto

Reprinted 1993 (Twice)

Photographs by David Mitton and Terry Permane
for Britt Allcroft's production of Thomas the Tank
Engine and Friends

ISBN 185591 247 3

Printed and bound in Great Britain by
BPCC Hazell Books, Paulton and Aylesbury

GORDON AND THE
FAMOUS VISITOR
buzz books

It was an important day in the yard.

Everyone was busy and excited, making notes and taking photographs. A special visitor had arrived and was now the centre of attention.

HE CITY OF TRURO'
3440 G.W.R.
3440
7

"Who's that?" whispered Thomas to Duck.

"That," said Duck proudly, "is a celebrity."

"A what?" asked Percy.

"A celebrity is a very famous engine," replied Duck. "Driver says we can talk to him soon."

"Oh," said Thomas. "He's probably too famous to even notice us."

Just then Gordon arrived.

"Pah," said Gordon. "Who cares? A lot of fuss about nothing if you ask me." And he steamed away.

Later that night, the engines found that the visitor wasn't conceited at all. He enjoyed talking to the other engines till long after the stars came out.

He left early next morning.

"Good riddance," Gordon grumbled. "Chattering all night. Who is he anyway?"

"Duck told you," said Thomas. "He's famous."

"As famous as me?" huffed Gordon. "Nonsense!"

"He's famouser than you," replied Thomas. "He went a hundred miles an hour before you were thought of."

"So he says," snorted Gordon. "But I didn't like his looks. He's got no dome. Never trust domeless engines. They're not respectable. I never boast, but I'd say that a hundred miles an hour would be easy for me."

1

Duck took some trucks to Edward's station.

"Hello," called Edward. "That famous engine came through this morning. He whistled to me. Wasn't he kind?"

"He's the finest engine in the world," replied Duck. Then he told Edward what Gordon had said.

"Take no notice," soothed Edward. "He's just jealous. Look! He's coming now."

4

Gordon's wheels pounded the rails.

"He did it! I'll do it. He did it! I'll do it."

Gordon's train rocketed past and was gone.

"He'll knock himself to bits," chuckled Duck.

"Steady, Gordon," called his driver. "We aren't running a race!"

"We are then," said Gordon, but he said it to himself. Suddenly Gordon began to feel a little strange. "The top of my boiler seems funny," he thought. "It feels as if something is loose. I'd better go slower."

But it was too late.

On the viaduct, they met the wind. It was a teasing wind which blew suddenly in hard puffs. Gordon thought it wanted to push him off the bridge.

4

"No you don't," he said firmly.

But the wind had other ideas. It curled around his boiler, crept under his loose dome and lifted it off and away into the valley below.

Gordon was most uncomfortable. The cold wind was whistling through the hole where his dome should be and he felt silly without it.

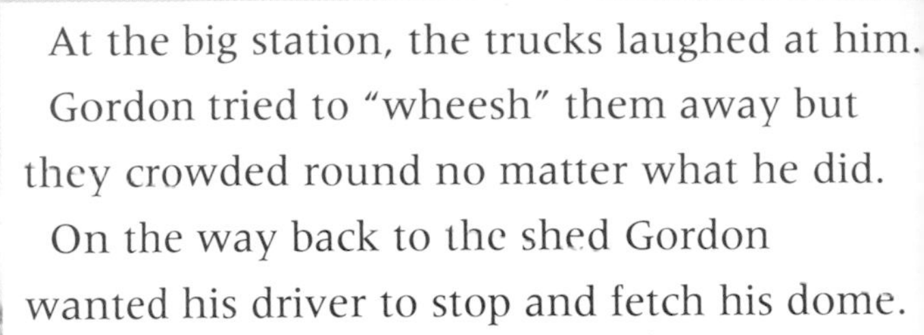

At the big station, the trucks laughed at him. Gordon tried to "wheesh" them away but they crowded round no matter what he did.

On the way back to the shed Gordon wanted his driver to stop and fetch his dome.

"We'll never find it now," said the driver. "You'll have to go to the works for a new one."

Gordon was very cross.

"I hope the shed is empty tonight," he huffed to himself.

But all the engines were there waiting.

"Never trust domeless engines," said a voice from somewhere behind him. "They aren't respectable."

THOMAS
1

EDWARD
2

GORDON
4